Disney

Olaf's FROZEN ADVENTURE

THEIR NEW HOLIDAY TRADITION

This book belongs to

_____

I began my new FROZEN tradition on

_____

© 2019 Disney Enterprises, Inc.

All rights reserved. Published by N & J Publishing. No part of this book may be reproduced or transmitted in any form or by any means, electronic or mechanical, including photocopying, recording, or by any information storage and retrieval system, without written permission from the publisher.

Manufactured in China

First Edition, Oct 2019

ISBN: 9780578502991

IT WAS TIME FOR THE HOLIDAYS in Arendelle, and the castle was buzzing with excitement. Queen Elsa and Princess Anna helped the castle staff decorate. It was their first holiday since Elsa became queen, and the sisters were throwing a surprise party for the entire kingdom. Olaf couldn't wait for the celebrations to begin. He popped out of a cake.

"SURPRISE!"

Anna giggled. "Olaf, not yet!"

Elsa smiled at the little snowman.

"Anna's right. Our surprise holiday party doesn't start until after the Yule Bell rings."

Soon townspeople filled the courtyard.
Kristoff and Sven wheeled in the giant Yule
Bell. As Anna and Elsa pulled the rope, the
bell's joyful sound rang out across the kingdom.
Elsa made the official announcement.
"LET THE HOLIDAYS BEGIN!"

As the doors to the castle opened, Anna signaled to Olaf.
"SURPRISE!"
But instead of entering the holiday party, all the townspeople started to walk away!

Anna rushed after them. "Wait! Wait! Wait! Hold on! Hold on! Going so soon?"

The villagers politely explained that they were going home to enjoy their family traditions. Besides, they didn't want to intrude on Anna and Elsa's traditions.

Kristoff tried to cheer up Anna and Elsa by sharing a tradition
that he and Sven had always enjoyed with the trolls. "It starts
with a gathering song, 'The Ballad of Flemmingrad.'"

Then Sven revealed a mud troll named Flemmy. Kristoff
demonstrated the final part of the tradition. "Now you lick his
forehead and make a wish."

But Anna and Elsa weren't about to lick the troll!

Kristoff shrugged. "Okay, not so much a royal activity, I get it.
But wait until you taste my traditional Flemmy stew! It may smell
like wet fur, but it's a real crowd-pleaser!"

Anna and Elsa followed Olaf into the ballroom. He wanted to know about their favorite family tradition. "What is it? Tell me! Tell me! Tell me!"

But Elsa could only remember ringing the Yule Bell. "After the gates were closed, we were never together. I'm sorry, Anna. IT'S MY FAULT WE DON'T HAVE A FAMILY TRADITION."

Anna watched sadly as Elsa left the room.

Olaf didn't like seeing Anna and Elsa so upset.

Suddenly, Olaf had an idea. He went to the stable to find Sven. "We'll go and find the best tradition Anna and Elsa have ever seen and bring it back to the castle! Are you with me?"

Together, the two friends hopped on Kristoff's sleigh to put Olaf's plan into motion. "LET'S GO FIND THEIR TRADITION!"

When they got to town, Olaf knocked on the first door he saw. Inside was a family who made candy canes together each year. They handed one to Olaf, and he replaced his carrot nose with it.

"Sugar rush!"

Olaf liked the family's tradition, but there were still many more to find!

As Olaf and Sven continued from house to house, the little snowman learned all about the different things families did together for the holidays.

He put something from every household onto the sleigh. Soon it was overflowing with wonderful traditions for Elsa and Anna!

It was nearly dark by the time they got to Wandering Oaken's Trading Post and Sauna. The large salesman greeted them at the door. "Hoo-hoo." Olaf and Sven joined the Oakens in their holiday tradition—relaxing in the family sauna. Oaken smiled at Olaf. "Enjoying the Christmas sweats, inquisitive magic snowman?"

Olaf nodded as he began to dissolve. "My troubles are just melting away."

Oaken tossed Olaf back out into the cold, where the snowman re-formed. He then happily threw a sauna onto the sleigh.

Pleased with all the traditions they had found, Sven and Olaf headed back to the castle. As they made their way through the woods, a hot coal from the sauna tumbled out and fell into the pile of traditions. THE WHOLE SLEIGH CAUGHT FIRE!

The burning sleigh dragged Olaf and Sven down the mountainside. They were flung to opposites sides of a ravine as the sleigh flew over a cliff. It exploded in the snow below. All the traditions were gone . . . EXCEPT ONE. Olaf triumphantly held up a fruitcake. "These things are indestructible."

The snowman told Sven he'd meet him back at the castle. He skipped into the dark woods.

In the distance, Sven heard the howling of hungry wolves chasing Olaf. He raced back toward the castle to get help.

Back at the castle, Elsa felt bad about walking away from Anna. She went to look for her sister. Elsa found Anna in the attic. "What are you doing up here?"

"Looking for traditions!"

Anna had been looking through her old trunk from her childhood. She wanted to know what was in Elsa's trunk.

Elsa shrugged. "Oh, mostly gloves."

Anna laughed, thinking her sister was joking, but when she looked in Elsa's trunk, it was true! "Oh." Elsa lifted a row of gloves and smiled slyly to herself as she spotted something. She reached into her trunk and pulled out a small wooden box with two tiny bells on it. She handed it to Anna.

Anna was confused. "What's that?"

Elsa smiled. "Look inside."

Anna opened the box, and her face brightened.

Meanwhile, Sven had arrived back at the castle. He burst into the stables and tried to tell Kristoff that Olaf was in danger, but Kristoff didn't understand. Anna and Elsa appeared in the doorway. They instantly knew what Sven was trying to say.

Anna was shocked. "Olaf's lost in the forest?"

Elsa gasped. "And being chased by hungry wolves?"

Anna took charge. "Ring the bell! GATHER EVERYONE!"

Anna, Elsa, Kristoff, Sven, and an Arendelle search party
headed into the mountains in search of Olaf. Anna and Elsa
called for their friend.

"Olaf?"

"Olaf, where are you?"

Suddenly, the sisters heard a sad, familiar voice. "He's not here."

Anna and Elsa looked down to see a carrot sticking out of a
large pile of snow. They shared a smile.

After Sven pulled Olaf out of the snow, Olaf told them everything that had happened. He'd lost everything he had gathered—even the fruitcake! "I'm sorry. You still don't have a tradition."

Anna shook her head. "But we do, Olaf. Look." Anna held the box open. Inside was artwork that she had made as a child for Elsa. THE ARTWORK WAS ALL OF OLAF!

Elsa smiled. "You were the one who brought us TOGETHER and kept us connected when we were APART."

Anna explained that she made artwork of Olaf for Elsa and slipped it under Elsa's door every year. Elsa had kept it all in a box.

The sisters both treasured the artwork, because it reminded them of their childhood and of how much they loved each other.

Anna and Elsa had a holiday tradition after all.
"IT'S YOU, OLAF. YOU ARE OUR TRADITION."
Olaf was delighted and surprised. "Me?"
Anna and Elsa gave Olaf a great big hug. The little
snowman giggled happily.

Kristoff, Sven, and the rest of the search party gathered around them. Everyone was overjoyed to see Olaf safe and sound. Elsa wanted to do something special to celebrate.

Using her magic, Elsa created a sparkling ice tree and decorated it with lanterns from the search party. She also made a star of ice around Anna's small Olaf sculpture. Then the little snowman hung it on top of the tree.

Elsa and Anna were happy and grateful to
be with family and friends.

Elsa looked around. "Well, I think Arendelle
has a new tradition."

Anna nodded. "Thank you, Olaf."